P9-DCQ-454

The Basket Ball

By Esmé Raji Codell ✫ Illustrated by Jennifer Plecas

Abrams Books for Young Readers
New York

The illustrations in this book were created with ink,
watercolor, and gouache on watercolor paper.

Cataloging-in-Publication Data has been applied for
and may be obtained from the Library of Congress.
ISBN 978-1-4197-0007-1

Printed and bound in China
10 9 8 7 6 5 4 3 2 1

Abrams Books for Young Readers are available at special
discounts when purchased in quantity for premiums and
promotions as well as fundraising or educational use. Special
editions can also be created to specification. For details, contact
specialsales@abramsbooks.com or the address below.

ABRAMS
THE ART OF BOOKS SINCE 1949
115 West 18th Street
New York, NY 10011
www.abramsbooks.com

To dear Pa, a good sport and a great dad
— E. R. C.

For Jelena, Nikola, Mile, and Jasmina
— J. P.

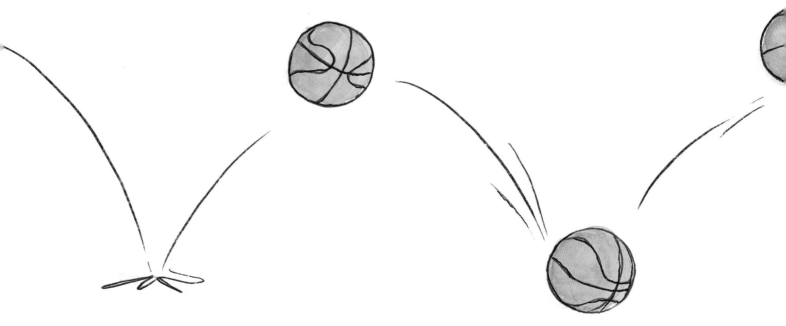

*L*ulu served with tea sets.

Lulu dressed in dresses.

Lulu's stuffed toy animals received her fond caresses.

Lulu messed with makeup.

Lulu played with dolls.

But most of all, our Lulu liked to shoot her basketballs.

Lulu, she could rebound.

Lulu, she could score.

Lulu was a vision as she shot across the floor.

Lulu was a winner, a championship dream.
Alas, alack! There were no girls
On Lulu's school-yard team.

"Girls cannot play," the guard would say,
Asserting his offensive.
"We'd knock you down, and doctor's bills
Are dreadfully expensive."

Lulu could have fought, but no, our Lulu did not quibble.
She offered up a hanky for the captain's double dribble.
"If there's no room for me," she said, "so much the worse for you.
If you won't let me join your team, there's one thing left to do.

"I'll send out invitations. Hear ye, hear ye, one and all:
Teamless girls from coast to coast . . ."

The word soon traveled around the globe
To go-to girls with game,

To step up to the three-point line
And try to earn their fame.

The girls arrived with coaches,
Jerseys sequined for the fete.

Their high-top heels glowed like fireflies,
Their hair wrapped in nothing but net.

The tip-off began with a whistle and grunt,
And the teams were on their feet,
No girl too refined for the passes and steals
That make scoreboards overheat.

The girls were ablaze! They crossed over! Slam-dunked!

How they jostled and shouted and played,

Laid up only for a sip of punch
That was mostly Gatorade.

Lulu examined the battle royal
With an eye out for talent in the midst of the fray,
But instead of uncovering a single star,
She discovered the Milky Way.

At the overtime buzzer, the players awaited
The verdict in sweat and in towel.
"My back's to the backboard, my friends." Lulu shrugged.
"To show favor would simply be foul."

"Then the answer is clear," came a voice from above,
As a girl six foot seven stepped forward and center.
"What we need is a league to play in year after year
And add spice to each season. Lulu girl, you're our mentor!
We're so glad we decided to answer your call
To assist at your very first Basket Ball."

Lulu became captain of
A lulu of a team.

Lulu now loses her hoop skirt
In lieu-lieu of her new hoop dream.

Glossary

How many of these basketball words and expressions can you find in the story?

ASSIST: *when the ball is passed to a teammate who scores*

BACKBOARD: *a large rounded or rectangular piece behind the hoop, usually made of wood or Plexiglas*

CENTER: *the player who's positioned closest to the basket—usually the tallest player; often blocks shots and scores*

COAST-TO-COAST: *taking the ball at one end of the court and scoring at the other end*

CROSSOVER: *faking out your opponent by pretending to move in one direction, then bouncing the ball between your legs and pivoting in the other direction instead*

DEFENSE: *trying to prevent the other team from scoring points*

DRIBBLE: *bouncing the ball up and down, which must be done at all times unless passing or shooting*

DOUBLE DRIBBLE: *when a player dribbles the ball, stops and holds it, and then dribbles again. A violation!*

FORWARD: *a position between the center and guard; usually a strong rebounder*

FOUL: *a penalty that is called when the referee decides there has been rough handling of one player by another*

FREE THROW: when a player is fouled, she may go to a designated line in front of the hoop and take one, two, or three shots (determined by the referee) without any defense in her way

GO-TO GIRL: a player with a history of making game-winning shots

GUARD: the position farthest from the basket; usually gets the most assists

JUMP BALL: when two players both have their hands on the ball, the referee stops the action and possession is decided by this special tip-off

LAYUP: a shot made very close to the basket, usually with the ball touching the backboard

NOTHING BUT NET: when the basketball goes through the hoop without touching the rim or the backboard. *Swish!*

OFFENSE: trying to score points

OVERTIME: additional time added to the game if the score at the end is tied

PASS: throwing the ball from one teammate to another

POSSESSION: getting the ball and keeping it away from the other team

REBOUND: getting the ball after an unsuccessful attempt has been made to score

REFEREE: the person who judges whether everybody is playing within the rules and playing safely, and whose decisions throughout the game stop and start the action

RIM: the structure from which the net hangs

SCOUT: someone looking for a talented player in order to hire or choose that person

SHOT CLOCK VIOLATION: a team has a set amount of time in which to shoot the ball once it gains possession; if the team does not shoot and at least hit the rim before its time runs out, the other team automatically gets the ball

SLAM DUNK: delivering the ball through the hoop while holding on to the ball. Not many girls and women can leap high enough to do this!

STEAL: when a member of one team takes the ball from a member of the other team

THREE-POINT LINE: if a player makes a shot at or beyond this line, the team earns three points instead of two

TIP-OFF: at the beginning of the game or at the beginning of overtime, the referee tosses the ball straight in the air and the centers try to tap the ball to a team member

TRAVEL: when a player tries to move the ball across the court without dribbling it. A violation!

VIOLATION: a mistake that results in the other team getting the ball